This book belongs to

For Edward, Rose, Freddie, Rory and Lily

Quarto is the authority on a wide range of topics.

Quarto educates, entertains and enriches the lives of our readers—enthusiasts and lovers of hands-on living.

www.quartoknows.com

This edition first published in 2018 by words & pictures,
an imprint of The Quarto Group.
The Old Brewery, 6 Blundell Street,
London N7 9BH, United Kingdom.
T (0)20 7700 6700 F (0)20 7700 8066
www.QuartoKnows.com

A catalogue record for this book is available from the British Library.

ISBN 978 1 78603 350 5

Manufactured in Guangdong, China CC042018

9 8 7 6 5 4 3 2 1

HAVE YOU HEARD?

Hannah Dale

words & pictures

The wood is quiet in the middle of the night,

A twig goes 'SNAP!'

…and wakes Mouse
with a fright!

"Have you heard,
sleepy, slimy frog,
That little sound
over by the log?

You don't think… could it be?
The big red fox is looking for…

ME?"

"Have you heard,
sweet sparrow, my dear?

Mouse heard the fox and he's ever so near!
While all us animals and birds are sleeping,
In the dark of the night he's softly creeping."

"Have you heard the slimy frog's warning?
The big red fox is out hunting this morning!

And silky squirrel,
you have never seen,
A cunning fox that's
quite as mean."

"Have you heard the news, old owl?
There's a fox in the wood
and he's on the prowl!

We're not even safe
up here in our tree.
I heard he can climb,
JUST LIKE ME!"

“Have you heard,
and are you wary?
There’s a fox in the wood,
who’s big and scary!
I heard his teeth are
pointy and sharp,
And even worse…

…HE CAN SEE IN THE DARK!”

“Have you heard,
big, bushy brown hare?
The fox has left his
underground lair!

I know you're fast, but then again...
I heard he's faster than a speeding train!"

“Have you heard that terrible growl?
The fox is hunting tasty fowl!

You can't escape so don't even try,
He has magic paws and I heard...

HE CAN FLY!"

"Have you heard that rumbling tummy?
The fox is looking for something yummy.

His claws are like
needles, his eyes
shine like lights
And he'll eat you up
in THREE BIG
BITES!"

"Have you heard what everyone says?
The fox is about and he's coming this way...

His claws are like needles,
His teeth are so sharp,
His eyes shine like lights...
He can see in the dark!

He can climb, he can run,
He's as big as the sun!
He's clever... he's sly...
He has wings... he can fly..."

"HAVE YOU HEARD?"

...not a word.